Pet Parade

Katie
the Kitten Fairy

Bella
the Bunny Fairy

The Pet
Fairies

Georgia
the Guinea Pig Fairy

Lauren
the Puppy
Fairy

Harriet
the Hamster
Fairy

Penny
the Pony Fairy

Molly
the Goldfish
Fairy

ISBN 978-0-545-46297-6

10 9 8 7 6 5 4 3 2 1   13 14 15 16 17/0

Printed in the U.S.A. 40
First printing, June 2013

Pet Parade

by Daisy
Meadows

SCHOLASTIC INC.

The Pet Fairies are enjoying a sunny day with their pets.

A pretty tune floats through the forest,
and a tiny blue bird flies into the clearing.
It's Flit!

Flit is a royal messenger.

He drops a red envelope into Bella's hands.

She opens it and reads the note.

"The king and queen need our help," Bella announces. "They want an animal friend of their very own!"

What is the best pet for the fairy king and queen?

"They must get a loyal goldfish," Molly says.

"No, they want a cuddly hamster," Harriet insists.

The Pet Fairies cannot agree.

"Let's take lots of pets to the palace,"
Georgia suggests. "Then the king and
queen can pick the perfect one."
"It will be a pet parade!" Katie exclaims.

The first stop is a barnyard.
Two ponies join Penny's in a grassy green field.

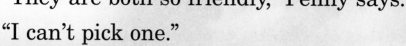

"They are both so friendly," Penny says.
"I can't pick one."
Penny takes both ponies.

Katie opens the tall, red barn doors.
A litter of kittens romps in the hay.
"They are too cute!" says Katie. "I can't
pick just one."
She lifts four kittens in her arms and
puts them in the cart.

Behind the barn, Harriet finds hamsters.

"They are all so furry," Harriet says.

She gently places three hamsters in a crate.

"The king and queen can choose," she says.

Bella sees the bunnies nearby.

They have long, silky ears and pink noses.

Bella gathers as many bunnies as she can carry.

Georgia cannot pick just one pet, either!
She giggles as she puts six guinea pigs in
a wagon.

Next, they visit a nearby stream.
Molly holds out a large glass bowl.

Three glittery goldfish leap out of the water.
They land in Molly's bowl with a *splash*.

The last stop is a toadstool cottage.
A pack of puppies tumbles in the grass.
The puppies lick Lauren's legs.

She lifts four playful puppies into the wagon.

At last, they are headed to Fairyland Palace.

One pony pulls the cart.

The other pulls the wagon.

The ponies are pulling a lot of pets!
"I wonder which pet the king and queen
will pick," Penny says.

All at once, a kitten jumps right into the
bunny crate.
A bunny bounds onto a pony's back.

The pony bolts forward, and the animals all charge through the palace gate.

The other pony jumps over a fountain, the wagon comes loose, and the goldfish spill into the pool!

The king and queen huddle in the middle of the palace garden.
The animals run, hop, and gallop around them.

"This isn't a parade," declares Katie. "It's a stampede!"

"What should we do?" cries Bella.

"Maybe we need a magic spell," suggests Lauren.

But then a sweet song rises above the
squeaks, barks, and whinnies.
Flit swoops around the animals.
The animals stop in their tracks.

Flit chirps a new song.

He flies in a straight line, and the animals follow.

The ponies, puppies, and kittens march.

The bunnies hop.
The guinea pigs and hamsters scramble
behind.
The goldfish do flips in the fountain.

The king and queen clap.

"Thank you, Pet Fairies," the king exclaims.

"What a grand pet parade."

"The animals are all cute," the queen says,

"but the king and I cannot agree on one pet."

The Pet Fairies gasp.

"We would like them all to be our animal friends," the king explains.

"We promise to give them a safe, happy home," adds the queen.

The Pet Fairies think it sounds like a great decision.

"We'd also like to thank Flit," the queen says. "He was a great help."

"Yes," says the king. "Flit will always be our special friend."

"Hooray for friends!" everyone cheers.

They all can agree on that!